BUM

Maggie M. Cooper

Illustrated by

Tyler Helms

another quality book by:
LEGACY Book Publishing
1883 Lee Road, Winter Park, FL 32789
(407) 647-3787 or (888)498-7887
LegacyBookPublishing.com

Inspired by the writing of Hazel Prowell Thompson

Dedicated to Mary Evans, Whit, and Hazel.
May you always choose to see that
beautiful hearts are what count most.

Published by:
LEGACY Book Publishing
1883 Lee Road
Winter Park, Florida 32789
LegacyBookPublishing.com
(407) 647-3787

ISBN: 978-1-947718-07-4
Printed in USA

Story by Maggie M. Cooper
Cover art and inside illustrations by Tyler Helms
Cover design by Gabriel H. Vaughn

Near the Big Swamp, down deep in the woods, lived a kind little frog named Bumper.
He was brave and strong and known for being a super long jumper.

He usually had a smile on his face, but lately he looked very glum.
His friends had been invited to play and most chose not to come.

You see, the other frogs decided Bumper was just too strange.
They liked things the way they were and didn't want to change.

He didn't like to sing in choir and harmonize with friends.
He would rather play guitar with old frogs in his den.

Instead of staying in the bog like his mom and dad,
He dreamed of being world famous jumping lily pads!

He didn't want to catch and eat the ordinary bugs.
He chose instead to dine on slug soup in silly mugs.

But most of all, Bumper chose to walk a different road,
Because his best friend Hazel was a bumpy, lumpy TOAD!

The other frogs made fun of her dry, bumpy skin,
Then gloated about their sleek, shiny coats with all their friends.

They gazed at their reflections and batted their big, beautiful eyes,
Then snickered at Hazel's squinty little slits when she would try.

The racing contest always drew lots of laughs and jeers.
The graceful frogs made Hazels' little hops leave her in tears.

But Bumper saw something special that the others didn't see.
He saw her heart and thought, "She's really just the same as me!"

We both love the water, have four legs and sticky tongues.
We both eat bugs, jump around, and play with everyone!

So though his heart was heavy when the others left them out,
He chose to play with Hazel and they'd laugh and play and shout!

They hopped over logs, hunted for bugs, and jumped from stone to stone.
They created funny leaf costumes and performed in the woods alone.

They collected worms to feed the fish and sunbathed on the bank.
They thought up funny schemes and played a lot of silly pranks.

One day after performing Romeo and Juliet,
Hazel heard a desperate cry, "Help! Somebody help!"

She rushed to find a little tadpole caught in a fisher's net.
She jumped right in and said, "Don't worry now! Don't fret!"

She pulled the little fella out and brought him back to safety.
The mama frog arrived and found a TOAD had saved her baby!

After seeing Hazel's kindness and courage on display,
A heart change occurred in the other frogs that day.

They looked at Hazel and didn't see her bumpy, lumpy skin.
They saw instead a friendly toad who made them laugh and grin.

They realized what Bumper had been saying all along.
The inside's what counts most and they had been so very wrong!

They stopped their jumping contest cold and made their way to them.
They asked to be forgiven and said, "Would you please be our friends?"

Hazel looked at Bumper and she said, "Is this for real?!?"
Then they both began to smile and hop and scream, "Of course we will!"

From that day on, the toads and frogs became the best of friends.
They realized they were more alike than different in the end.

"...The Lord doesn't see things the way you see them. People judge by outward appearance, but the Lord looks at the heart."
—1 Samuel 16:7 NLT